BEWARE, BEAK!
I, DR. HEINZ DOOFENSHMIRTZ,
WILL BE THE ULTIMATE
SUPERVILLAIN TO BATTLE YOU
FOR CONTROL OF THE
TRI-STATE AREA!

ADAPTED BY JOHN GREEN

BASED ON THE SERIES CREATED BY
DAN POVENMIRE & JEFF "SWAMPY" MARSH

Disney PRESS

NEW YORK

ISBN 978-1-4231-3740-5
FIRST EDITION
10 9 8 7 6 5 4 3 2 1
PRINTED IN THE UNITED STATES OF AMERICA
H886-4759-0-11227

FOR MORE DISNEY PRESS FUN, VISIT WWW.DISNEYBOOKS.COM
VISIT DISNEYCHANNEL.COM

SUMMER VACATION! THERE'S A WHOLE LOT OF STUFF TO DO BEFORE SCHOOL STARTS, AND **PHINEAS** AND **FERB** PLAN TO DO IT ALL! MAYBE THEY'LL BUILD A ROCKET, OR FIND FRANKENSTEIN'S BRAIN...WHATEVER THEY DO, THEY'RE SURE TO ANNOY THEIR SISTER, **CANDACE**. MEANWHILE, THEIR FAMILY PET, **PERRY** THE PLATYPUS, LEADS A DOUBLE LIFE AS **AGENT P**, FACING OFF AGAINST THE DEVIOUS **DR. DOOFENSHMIRTZ!**

"THE BEAK STRIKES!"

HERE IT IS:
THE PHINEAS AND FERB EDGE-OF-INSANITY-KISS-YOUR-BUTT-GOOD-BYE-GRAVITY'S-A-STONE-COLD-SUCKER-NIGHTMARE-RAIL-SKATE-TRACK OBSTACLE COURSE OF *DOOM*.

YOU READY, FERB?

OOPS.

GAH!

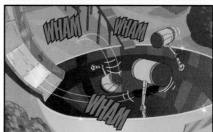

OOOH!

RRAHWR!

OUCH!

BOOM!

YOU KNOW, IT OCCURS TO ME, WE COULD GET *HURT*. I GUESS THE "OF DOOM" IN THE NAME SHOULD HAVE TIPPED US OFF. WELL, FERBOOCH, UNFORTUNATELY, THERE'S ONLY ONE WAY DOWN.

THE STAIRS.

MEANWHILE...

MOM! PHINEAS AND FERB HAVE BUILT A GIANT SKATEBOARD OBSTACLE COURSE OF DOOM ON TOP OF THE HOUSE! YOU HAVE TO--

CANDACE? OH, YOU HAVE **GOT TO** BE KIDDING ME. IF YOU HADN'T NOTICED, I'M KIND OF IN THE **MIDDLE** OF SOMETHING HERE.

BUT MOM--

OUT!

ALL RIGHT, ALL RIGHT, **JEEZ,** DON'T TAKE IT OUT ON ME. **I'M** THE GOOD GUY HERE!

OKAY, LET'S GET BACK TO YOUR ROOT CANAL.

AH, THANK GOODNESS.

BACK AT THE HOUSE...

HI, PHINEAS. I'M GOING FOR MY "INTREPID REPORTER" PATCH. CAN I REPORT ON WHAT **YOU** GUYS ARE DOING?

SURE!

COOL. ISABELLA GARCIA-SHAPIRO, THE **FIRESIDE GIRLS GAZETTE,** WHAT'CHA DOOOOIN'?

FERB AND I HAVE BUILT THE ULTIMATE EXTREME SKATE-TRACK OBSTACLE COURSE.

AWESOME! I **KNEW** I COULD COUNT ON YOU FOR THE COOLEST STORY **EVER.** HAVE YOU ATTEMPTED A RUN YET?

WELL, WE DECIDED WE NEED TO MAKE A FEW TWEAKS AND ADJUSTMENTS.

SO WE CAN, YOU KNOW, **SURVIVE** AND STUFF.

OKAY, I'LL BE BACK. HOPEFULLY, I CAN MAKE THE EARLY MIDMORNING EDITION.

SEE YA!

HMM, INSTEAD OF MODIFYING THE **TRACK,** MAYBE WE SHOULD MODIFY **OURSELVES.**

TOGETHER WE COULD BE THE MOST ULTIMATE SKATEBOARDER **EVER!**

HEY, WHERE'S PERRY?

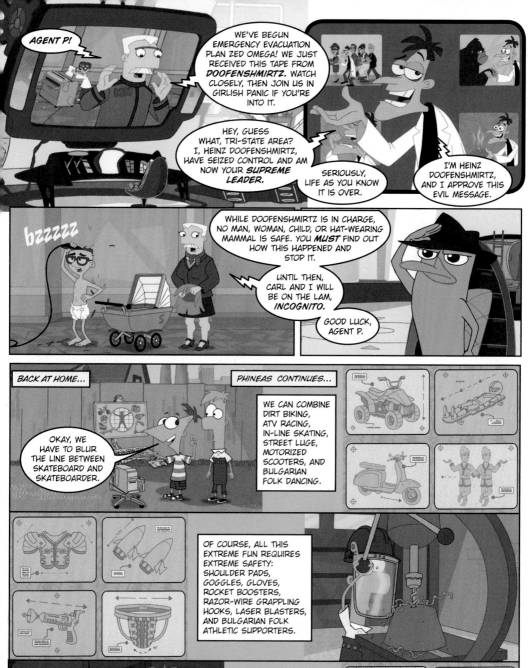

AGENT P!

WE'VE BEGUN EMERGENCY EVACUATION PLAN ZED OMEGA! WE JUST RECEIVED THIS TAPE FROM **DOOFENSHMIRTZ.** WATCH CLOSELY, THEN JOIN US IN GIRLISH PANIC IF YOU'RE INTO IT.

HEY, GUESS WHAT, TRI-STATE AREA? I, HEINZ DOOFENSHMIRTZ, HAVE SEIZED CONTROL AND AM NOW YOUR **SUPREME LEADER.**

SERIOUSLY, LIFE AS YOU KNOW IT IS OVER.

I'M HEINZ DOOFENSHMIRTZ, AND I APPROVE THIS EVIL MESSAGE.

bzzzzz

WHILE DOOFENSHMIRTZ IS IN CHARGE, NO MAN, WOMAN, CHILD, OR HAT-WEARING MAMMAL IS SAFE. YOU **MUST** FIND OUT HOW THIS HAPPENED AND STOP IT.

UNTIL THEN, CARL AND I WILL BE ON THE LAM, **INCOGNITO.**

GOOD LUCK, AGENT P.

BACK AT HOME...

PHINEAS CONTINUES...

OKAY, WE HAVE TO BLUR THE LINE BETWEEN SKATEBOARD AND SKATEBOARDER.

WE CAN COMBINE DIRT BIKING, ATV RACING, IN-LINE SKATING, STREET LUGE, MOTORIZED SCOOTERS, AND BULGARIAN FOLK DANCING.

OF COURSE, ALL THIS EXTREME FUN REQUIRES EXTREME SAFETY: SHOULDER PADS, GOGGLES, GLOVES, ROCKET BOOSTERS, RAZOR-WIRE GRAPPLING HOOKS, LASER BLASTERS, AND BULGARIAN FOLK ATHLETIC SUPPORTERS.

THEN, WE LOCK IT ALL TOGETHER WITH AN INDESTRUCTIBLE TITANIUM EXOSKELETON THAT INCREASES STRENGTH, JUMPING ABILITY, AND OTHER PHYSICAL ATTRIBUTES ONE HUNDRED TIMES, INCLUDING THE SENSES AND FOLK-DANCING ABILITY.

WHAT? YOU THINK WE SHOULD HAVE *MORE* BULGARIAN FOLK-RELATED ELEMENTS?

OH, *LESS?*

LESS. OKAY. WOW. I THOUGHT WE WERE ON THE SAME PAGE, BUT NO, IT'S COOL. WHATEVER.

TIME TO SUIT UP!

LET'S START WITH THE BASICS.

FINGERS FUNCTIONAL!

beep

FEET FUNCTIONAL!

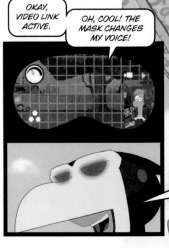

OKAY, VIDEO LINK ACTIVE.

OH, COOL! THE MASK CHANGES MY VOICE!

OH, YEAH. HOW ABOUT A LITTLE TEST DRIVE?

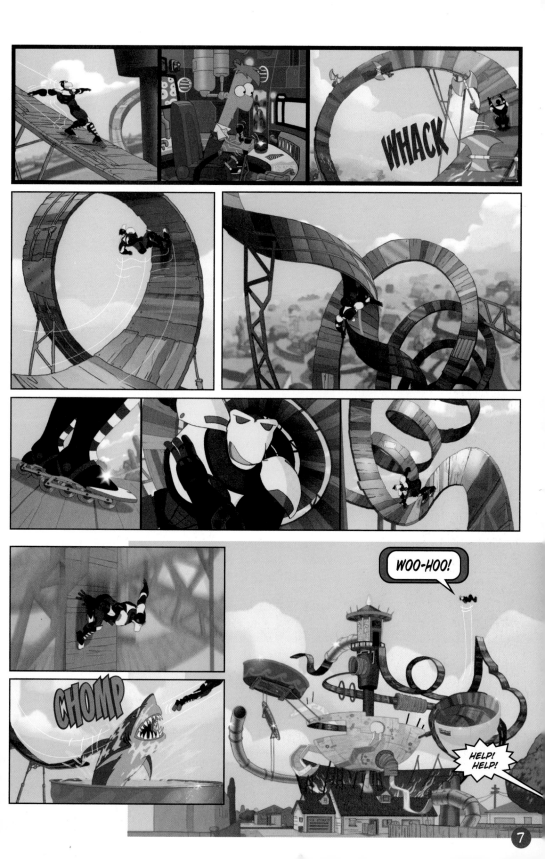

WAIT! IN THE DISTANCE, DO YOU HEAR THAT?

HELP! HE'S STUCK IN THE TREE, AND I CAN'T GET HIM DOWN!

SOUNDS LIKE BUFORD'S IN TROUBLE. HEY, FERB, MAYBE WE CAN USE THE SUIT TO HELP HIM.

HOLD ON TIGHT!

HIT THE ROCKET BOOSTERS.

FWOOSH

WHOA!

YEAH!

HEY, FERB, CHECK US OUT. WE'RE FLYING!

PHINEAS, I'M BACK.

PHINEAS? FERB?

WELL, I GUESS THERE GOES MY STORY.

HELP, MY NERD IS STUCK IN A TREE!

LOOK, THERE THEY ARE!

MEANWHILE...

IT'S *NOT* FAIR! EVERY TIME I TRY TO BUST PHINEAS AND FERB, IT'S, "CANDACE, I'M SHOPPING." "CANDACE, I'M HAVING ROOT CANAL SURGERY." "CANDACE, I'M DELIBERATING WITH A SEQUESTERED JURY. HOW'D YOU EVEN GET IN HERE?"

THEN MY-- OH, LOOK, A FLYING MAN.

WAIT A SECOND, ISN'T THAT *IMPOSSIBLE?*

WAIT *ANOTHER* SECOND, SOMETHING IMPOSSIBLE *PLUS* THAT THING EXISTING IN REAL LIFE EQUALS--

-:GASP!:-

PHINEAS AND FERB!

WELL, WE FIGURED OUT HOW TO FLY. NOW WE NEED TO FIGURE OUT HOW TO *STOP* FLYING.

DEPLOYING GRAPPLING HOOKS!

CLANK

CRUNCH

WELL, AT LEAST WE STOPPED FLYING.

MEANWHILE...

Doofenshmirtz Evil Inc.

EX-LEADERS OF THE TRI-STATE AREA, I HAVE CALLED YOU HERE TO HELP *EASE* THE PEOPLE THROUGH THIS TRANSITION OF POWER.

UM, I'M ONLY THE CROSSING GUARD AT FOURTH STREET AND MAPLE. I DON'T REALLY HAVE MUCH AUTHORITY.

AND I THOUGHT YOU CALLED ME HERE TO RECAULK YOUR TUB.

SILENCE! ARE YOU SUGGESTING IN MY ATTEMPT TO GATHER THE LEADERS OF THE TRI-STATE AREA THE BEST I COULD DO IS A CROSSING GUARD AND MY BUILDING SUPER?

YOU'RE *WRONG!*

YOU KNOW WHO *THAT* IS? IT'S ONLY ROGER DOOFENSHMIRTZ, THE *MAYOR* OF DANVILLE. WHAT DO *YOU* KNOW? YOU'RE ONLY A CROSSING GUARD.

I'M SORRY, BUT IF WE'RE NOT ACTUALLY GOING TO *PLAN* MOM'S BIRTHDAY PARTY, THEN I'VE GOT TO JET.

HEY-HEY WAIT, *WAIT.* COME BACK. I'M NOT--

OH, *GREAT,* PERRY THE PLATYPUS. THIS IS *ALL* I NEED. SO, WHAT DID YOU WANT TO TALK TO ME ABOUT?

WHAM!

OOMF!!

WHOA! WHOA! WHOA.

BACK AT THE HOUSE...

WOW, THE SUIT MAKES THE CLEANUP FAST, FUN, AND 'FFICIENT.

I FEEL BAD ABOUT MISSING ISABELLA, THOUGH.

I HOPE SHE FOUND SOMETHING ELSE TO WRITE A STORY ABOUT.

EARLY MIDMORNING EDITION! THE BEAK SAVES THE GEEK!

"SUPERHERO COMES TO DANVILLE. BY ISABELLA GARCIA-SHAPIRO. I CALL HIM *THE BEAK*."

HEY, I LIKE THAT!

GIRLS GAZETTE
Vol. 1, Issue 1
New Patch - page. 9

SUPERHERO COMES TO DANVILLE

by ISABELLA GARCIA-SHAPI

"WITH THE BEAK WATCHING OVER US, EVERYONE IN DANVILLE IS FREE TO HAVE THE BEST DAY EVER."

EVIL-DOERS BEWARE

ELSEWHERE...

"FREE TO HAVE THE BEST DAY EVER," HUH?

WE'LL SEE ABOUT *THAT*.

ARE YOU IN THERE COMPLAININ' AGAIN 'BOUT NEVER HAVIN' A GOOD DAY IN YOUR LIFE?

WELL, DEAR, I NEVER DID! WHERE'S *MY* BEST DAY EVER? THANK YOU VERY MUCH.

HA. I TOLD *HER*.

I HEARD THAT!

WHAM!

A *SUPERHERO?* THAT'S NOT AT *ALL* WHAT WE PLANNED TO DO TODAY.

riiiiing

OH, HI, ISABELLA.

PHINEAS, WHERE'D YOU *GO?* IT'S A GOOD THING SOMETHING ELSE CAME ALONG FOR ME TO REPORT ON, BUT YOU *REALLY* LET ME DOWN.

YEAH, *SORRY* ABOUT THAT. BUT HEY, MAYBE WE CAN MAKE IT UP TO YOU. HOW WOULD YOU LIKE AN *EXCLUSIVE?*

REALLY? *GREAT!* MEET ME DOWNTOWN IN FIVE MINUTES.

COME ON! WE HAVE TO GO TELL ISABELLA WE'RE *THE BEAK.*

-:AHEM:-

FINE, WE CAN TAKE THE SUIT.

WOOOSH

AH-HA! I *KNEW* IT WAS THE--

FWAP

OTHER NEWS

WARM WEATHER

"SUPERHERO COMES TO DANVILLE."

WELL, THEY'RE ABOUT TO GET *SUPERBUSTED.*

BEHOLD, THE KAKA-CRAWLER! I BUILT IT IN MY BASEMENT OUT OF DISCARDED WASHERS AND DRYERS, THANK YOU VERY MUCH.

AND I'M GONNA MAKE SURE NO ONE HAS THE BEST DAY EVER!

SAVE MY BABY!

PHINEAS, WHERE ARE YOU? THERE'S THIS GIANT ROBOT MACHINE ATTACKING DOWNTOWN DANVILLE!

I'M ALL ALONE HERE. CALL ME AS SOON AS YOU GET THIS.

COME ON, ISABELLA, THIS IS WHAT BEING AN INTREPID REPORTER IS ALL ABOUT.

OH, THIS IS NOT GOOD, MELANIE. I BET THEY'LL TRY TO PIN THIS ON ME.

YEAH, IT'S NOT LIKE YOU'RE THE ONE WHO USED THE UNSIGNED PROPOSAL FOR "DEFENDING DANVILLE FROM GIANT ROBOT ATTACKS" AS A COASTER.

OH, WAIT, YOU WERE.

YES, IT'S SO EASY TO BLAME THE GUY IN CHARGE.

-:GASP:-

THE GUY IN CHARGE! HA-HA! THAT'S IT!

MEANWHILE...

UH, YOU KNOW THAT WHOLE TAKING OVER THE TRI-STATE AREA THING? I-I-I WAS JUST BLUFFING. I-I HOPED MAYBE IF I JUST *TOLD* EVERYONE I WAS IN CHARGE, THEY'D BE TOO LAZY OR TOO BUSY TO, YOU KNOW, ACTUALLY *CHECK*.

riing

OH, HELLO, *ROGER.*

UH-HUH. WHAT? YOU ARE? *ME?* IN CHARGE? IT WORKED? YOU'RE KIDDING. YOU--YOU'RE *NOT* KIDDING?

BACK DOWNTOWN...

WHERE'S PHINEAS? HE'D KNOW WHAT TO DO.

WHO KNEW WRECKING EVERYBODY'S DAY WOULD BE THIS MUCH *FUN.*

WHAT'S GOING ON?

HEY, LOOK, THERE'S ISABELLA.

PRESS

THE BEAK!

YO, ISABELLA--

SLAP

TAKE *THAT,* BIRDBRAIN!

CRUNCH

SPROING!

SNAP

OH, *GREAT.* NOW I HAVE TO RESTART, THANK YOU VERY MUCH.

ZZZAAP!

DUDE, WHO *ARE* YOU, ANYWAY?

IF YOU'RE HERE TO GIVE DANVILLE THE *BEST* DAY EVER, THEN I'M HERE TO GIVE DANVILLE THE *WORST* DAY EVER.

YOU CAN CALL ME... *KAKAPOOPOO!*

HA HA HA
HA
HA HA HA

WHAT? OH, *COME ON!* IT'S A FAMILY NAME.

Gustav Khaka Peü Peü

LOOSELY TRANSLATED AS "THE STRONG FIST" OR "THAT STRONG FIST." *THANK YOU VERY MUCH!*

ALL RIGHT, LET'S WRAP THIS UP.

HEY, MY FIRST SUPERHERO PUN!

ISABELLA GARCIA-SHAPIRO, THE *FIRESIDE GIRLS GAZETTE.* WOULD IT BE OKAY IF I ASKED YOU A FEW QUESTIONS?

HUH?

UM, I CAN'T TALK RIGHT NOW. GOTTA GO, BYE.

OH, UH, OKAY. BYE. THANKS FOR SAVING ME.

WE CAN'T TELL ISABELLA WE'RE THE BEAK NOW; THAT WOULD PUT HER IN DANGER!

THE LIFE OF A SUPERHERO IS A LONELY ONE, FERB. EVEN AFTER ONLY ELEVEN MINUTES.

MEANWHILE, AT HOME, CANDACE HAS A PLAN...

ARE YOU SURE PHINEAS AND FERB ARE REALLY THE BEAK? HE'S JUST SO *HEROIC* AND *HUNKY.*

FIRESIDE GIRLS GAZETTE
SUPERHERO COMES TO DANVILLE

GAH! BARFARONI WITH CHEESE! STACY, *PLEASE.* PHINEAS AND FERB ARE DOING SOMETHING TOTALLY *BUSTABLE,* THAT'S *ALSO* MOBILE.

WE CAN *LURE* THEM RIGHT TO MOM TO BUST *THEMSELVES.*

AND HOW EXACTLY WILL *WE* DO THIS?

WELL, IF THEY WANNA PLAY SUPER-*HERO,* THEN WE'RE GONNA PLAY SUPER-*VILLAIN.*

CALL ME...*THE DANGERAFFE.*

RIGHT. AND WHERE DO I FIT IN?

YOU'LL BE MY HENCHMAN. IT'S LIKE THE BRIDESMAID OF CRIME.

OKAY, GOT IT.

ALTHOUGH, IT LOOKS LIKE THEY'VE GOT THEIR HANDS FULL WITH KAKAPOOPOO.

DOWNTOWN CLASH!

THAT'S OBVIOUSLY SOME BIG, STUPID DRESS-UP GAME THEY'RE PLAYING WITH THEIR LITTLE LOSER FRIENDS.

SUPERFELLOW!

NOW, IF MY RESEARCH IS CORRECT, THE WAY TO DEFEAT A SUPERHERO...

...IS TO COME AT HIM THROUGH WHAT'S IMPORTANT TO HIM. *MWA-HA-HA-HA!*

DOWNTOWN...

HEY, CHECK *THIS* PLACE OUT. SWANKY! MELANIE?

HELLO, HEINZ.

NO, NO, PLEASE CALL ME *SUPREME LEADER DOOFENSHMIRTZ THE GREAT.*

NO.

OH, I SEE ROGER LEFT ME A NOTE. LET'S SEE.

Bro,
Thanks for filling in for me! You're gonna make a *GREAT* Fall Guy.
I MEAN, MAYOR!!
—Roger

"BRO, THANKS FOR FILLING IN FOR ME. YOU'RE GONNA MAKE A *GREAT* FALL GUY. I MEAN, MAYOR!"

AW, THAT'S SO SWEET.

GO AHEAD AND PUT THAT ON MY NEW DESK.

SPROING!

HA-HA! MADE YOU CARRY YOUR OWN TRAP!

NOW, MY *FIRST* ORDER OF BUSINESS IS TO MAKE ALL THE CITIZENS OF DANVILLE *BOW DOWN*--

NO, IT'S NOT.

HERE'S YOUR SCHEDULE AND ALL YOUR MISSED PHONE CALLS. LET'S FOCUS.

OH, UH, *WOW,* UH, OKAY.

AND IN CASE YOU HADN'T NOTICED, THE CITY IS IN THE GRIP OF FEAR AND PANIC CAUSED BY AN EVIL SUPERVILLAIN INTENT ON DESTROYING OUR WAY OF LIFE.

DOWNTOWN CLASH!

WHAT? BUT-BUT THAT'S *MY* JOB!

BACK TO PHINEAS AND FERB...

THERE! YOU CAN'T EVEN TELL WE'VE BUILT OUR **SECRET LAIR** UP IN THE TREE.

HI, GUYS.

NOTHING!

I MEAN, HI, ISABELLA. WE'RE...NOT DOING...NOTHING.

WHERE HAVE YOU BEEN?

UM, OH, YOU KNOW US. BUSY, BUSY, BUSY.

RIGHT. WHILE YOU TWO WERE BUSY MAKING SURE YOUR SUMMER DAY WAS **FUN**, OTHER PEOPLE WERE BUSY **SAVING** DANVILLE.

AND I NEED **YOUR** HELP FINDING **THE BEAK.** I THOUGHT THERE MIGHT BE SOME CLUES IN THE PHOTOS I TOOK THAT COULD HELP HIM STOP KAKAPOOPOO.

-:CHUCKLE:-

FINE, IF YOU GUYS AREN'T GOING TO TAKE THIS SERIOUSLY, I'LL FIND THE BEAK ON MY **OWN.**

ISABELLA, WAIT.

I GOTTA GO. **BYE,** PHINEAS.

FERB...TO **THE NEST!**

VVVrrrrt

POP

CRACKLE

READY, FERB? LET'S **WING IT.**

FWOOSH

BA-CAW!

20

BACK DOWNTOWN...

HA-HA-HA-HA!

AAH! IT'S RAINING WORMS!

AND NOT THE GOOD KIND!

TIME TO CLEAN UP YOUR MESS, KAKAPOOPOO!

snap snap snap snap

GAZETTE
Vol.1, Issue 2
THE EARLY BIRD
by ISABELLA GARCIA-SHAPIRO
GETS THE WORM!

FLY, MY PRETTIES!

YOUR EVIL SCHEME WAS FOR THE BIRDS, KAKAPOOPOO!

snap snap snap

THE BEAK...WHO IS HE?

NEARBY...

PHINEAS, *QUICK!* MOM IS IN *DANGER!* AAAHH!! ON THE CORNER OF FOURTH STREET AND MAPLE DRIVE! *AAAAHHH!!!*

AND THE AWARD GOES TO...*ME!*

BEAUTIFUL.

NOW, IT'S ALL UP TO *THE DANGERAFFE!*

SO THEN, WHAT DOES *THE DANGERBIL** DO?

I TOLD YOU. YOU'RE MY HENCHMAN. *HENCH* OR SOMETHING.

*SHE'S IN A GERBIL BALL!

OH, *NO,* YOU DID *NOT* JUST TELL ME TO *HENCH.*

OKAY, JUST WATCH MY BIKE. I'LL BE RIGHT BACK.

MWAHA-HA-HA!

CANDACE, WHAT ON *EARTH* ARE YOU *DOING?*

GIVE, WOMAN!

WHAT DO YOU NEED? GUM?

HELP! HELP! I'M TAKING HER PURSE!

HERE, HONEY, HERE'S A TWENTY. WHY DON'T YOU GO SEE A MOVIE?

A-HA! I STOLE TWENTY BUCKS FROM THIS WOMAN! HELP! THE BEAK! *THE BEAK!*

HI, MOM. HI CANDACE. EVERYTHING OKAY?

WHAT? WHERE'S THE BEAK? MOM'S BEEN ROBBED!

OH, YES, RIGHT. APPARENTLY *GIRAFFE GIRL* HAS *ROBBED* ME.

OH, **COME ON.** ADMIT IT! YOU TWO ARE *SUPERHEROES.*

WELL, FERB *HAS* BEEN WORKING OUT. THANKS FOR NOTICING!

kiss

kiss

TELL HER THE *TRUTH.* YOU'RE MAKING ME LOOK *RIDICULOUS.*

WAY TOO EASY.

I LOST YOUR BIKE.

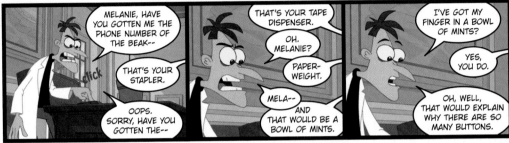

COME ON, FERB. LET'S GET BACK TO THE NEST.

OH, HELLO, FERB.

PHINEAS.

HEY, ISABELLA. SORRY WE HAD TO DUCK OUT ON YOU EARLIER.

WELL, THAT'S OKAY. IT'S JUST KINDA WEIRD FOR ME NOT TO KNOW WHERE YOU ARE OR *WHAT'CHA DOOOIN'*.

FAIR ENOUGH.

MS. GARCIA-SHAPIRO?

I'VE GOT YOUR NEXT HEADLINE:

EVERYBODY'S DAY RUINED ONCE AND FOR ALL, AND THE BEAK'S POWERLESS TO SAVE IT!

UM, IT'S A *LITTLE WORDY* FOR A HEADLINE.

ENOUGH! OKAY, DANVILLE. NOTHING RUINS A DAY FASTER THAN UNEXPECTED *RAIN SHOWERS!*

SPLOOSH!

YOU MONSTER! NOW I'M *WET!*

HA-HA-HA-HA-HA!

OH, NO! THIS IS **TERRIBLE!** I'M SO GLAD YOU'RE HERE WITH ME, PHINEAS. COME ON, WE CAN COVER THE ACTION BETTER FROM THE TOP OF CITY HALL.

PHINEAS?

I'M SORRY, ISABELLA. WE CAN'T GO WITH YOU.

YOU'RE GONNA LEAVE ME **AGAIN?**

YOU'RE GONNA HAVE TO TRUST ME. HAVE I EVER LET YOU DOWN?

YES! LIKE FOUR TIMES TODAY **ALONE.**

I'M SORRY, ISABELLA. MAYBE ONE DAY YOU'LL UNDERSTAND.

COME ON, FERB. **LET'S ROLL.**

PHINEAS! DON'T YOU LEAVE ME. **PHINEAS!**

SOON...

I GUESS YOUR **SUPERHERO** TURNED OUT TO BE A **CHICKEN** BEAK. BWAUK-BUK-BUK-BUK!

WELL, WHICH CAME FIRST...

...THE CHICKEN OR THE EGG?

FOOMP FOOMP

SPLAT

SPLAT

BLEARGH!

WELL, **I'VE** GOT A SURPRISE FOR **YOU,** TOO. I'M NOT **ALONE** THIS TIME. MAY I INTRODUCE...

GRAB!

THROW!

CRUNCH

POP!

WHOA!

HELP!

OH, NO! ISABELLA!

AND THAT'S NOT ALL, DO-GOODER.

WATCH AS I DESTROY THE VERY SYMBOL OF GOOD DAYS EVERYWHERE!

ZZZAAP.

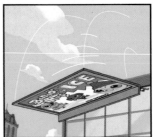

OH, NO! "BANGO-RUS ON ICE" WILL CRUSH US!

UH-OH! TWO PROBLEMS, ONE BEAK.

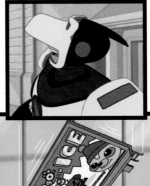

I CAN'T HOLD ON!

AAAHH!

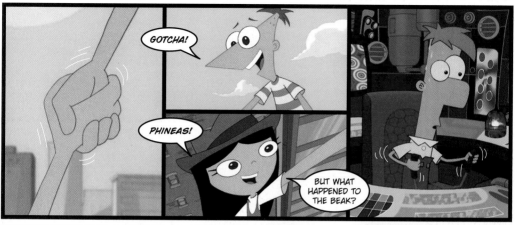

AGENT P JUMPS INTO THE BEAK SUIT!

WHAT?

CRUNCH

LEAP!

CURSE YOU, PERRY THE BEAKAPUS!

GOOD WORK, AGENT P.

OH, *HEY*, MY VISION'S CLEARING UP. SO, WHAT DID YOU WANT ME TO SEE?

OH, FORGET IT.

OKAY, THEN. WHY DON'T WE ALL GO HOME FOR SOME SNACKS?

BY THE WAY, PHINEAS, YOU WERE *VERY* BRAVE.

THANKS! YOU WERE TOO.

UM, *HELLO?* ENTIRE *LOWER HALF* OF AMAZING SUPERHERO HERE.

⇥SIGH⇤

I GUESS THERE'S NO GLORY IN *THIGHS*.

AND, SO, THINGS PRETTY MUCH WORKED OUT, I GUESS. NARRATOR GUY IS OUT. *PEACE!*